NIGEL HINTON

BEAVER TOWERS

THE FIRST BOOK IN THE BEAVER TOWERS SERIES

Illustrated by Anne Sharp

PUFFIN BOOKS

For Syb

PUFFIN BOOKS

Published by the Penguin Group
Penguin Books Ltd, 80 Strand, London WC2R 0RL, England
Penguin Putnam Inc., 375 Hudson Street, New York, New York 10014, USA
Penguin Books Australia Ltd, 250 Camberwell Road, Camberwell, Victoria 3124, Australia
Penguin Books Canada Ltd, 10 Alcorn Avenue, Toronto, Ontario, Canada M4V 3B2
Penguin Books India (P) Ltd, 11 Community Centre, Panchsheel Park, New Delhi – 110 017, India
Penguin Books (NZ) Ltd, Cnr Rosedale and Airborne Roads, Albany, Auckland, New Zealand
Penguin Books (South Africa) (Pty) Ltd, 24 Sturdee Avenue, Rosebank 2196, South Africa

Penguin Books Ltd, Registered Offices: 80 Strand, London WC2R 0RL, England

www.penguin.com

First published by Abelard-Schuman Limited 1980
Published in Puffin Books 1995

030

Text copyright © Nigel Hinton, 1980
Illustrations copyright © Anne Sharp, 1995
All rights reserved

Set in 11/14 pt Monophoto Ehrhardt by Rowlands Phototypesetting Ltd, Bury St.Edmunds, Suffolk

Printed in England by Clays Ltd, St Ives plc

British Library Cataloguing in Publication Data
A CIP catalogue record for this book is available from the British Library

ISBN-13: 978-0-14-037060-7

www.greenpenguin.co.uk

CHAPTER ONE

Maybe none of it would have happened if Philip had listened to his father's warning not to play with the kite on his own. Maybe. But who can tell with magic?

'It's big enough to blow you away,' his mother said when she saw the kite.

Philip laughed. Nobody had ever been blown away on a kite – not even on one as huge as this. His uncle had brought it back as a present from China and it really was the biggest and best you've ever seen. It was shaped like a dragon and was coloured red, yellow and green.

Philip wanted to go out and fly it at once but his father said he had to wait until the weekend. The weekend! That was four whole days away.

Philip put the kite in the corner of his bedroom. Every time he looked at it, he heard a voice whispering in his head.

'Go on,' the voice said, 'it's your kite. Dad's just a spoil-sport. Go on – it'll be good fun. No one will know if you just sneak out for half an hour.'

For two days Philip managed to say 'no' to the voice, but on the third day he gave in.

He picked up the kite and opened his bedroom door as quietly as possible. He tiptoed down the stairs. His mother was working at her desk in the front room and he knew that she could see the street from there, so he went out of the side door and along the alley-way at the back of the house.

The kite was so big that his arms ached from holding it up so that it didn't touch the ground. It was so big that by the time he reached the top of the hill in the park he was out of breath.

Then, after all that, there wasn't even the slightest breeze. For a quarter of an hour, he ran up and down trying to make the kite fly, but each time it just flapped back to the ground. After one final go, he gave up. He wrapped the string into a ball and bent down to pick up the kite. A little puff of wind blew his hair. He looked up. A small, round, black cloud was racing across the blue sky. It was moving faster than any cloud Philip had ever seen. He felt the kite move in his hand. The long dragon's tail wagged from side to side like a dog's when it sees a friend.

The cloud got nearer and nearer the sun. Philip

saw its shadow come racing up the hill towards him. It grew darker and Philip waited for the shadow to pass. But when he looked up, the cloud had stopped, directly in front of the sun. Its shadow formed a perfect circle all round him.

Then, out of nowhere came the wind. Whistling and spinning and howling. Philip closed his eyes. He felt his arms rise up above him as the wind caught the kite and lifted it. For a moment, he thought of letting go but there was a sudden tug and it was too late. When he opened his eyes, he was already twenty feet above the ground and rising fast. Straight up. He watched the top of the hill grow smaller and smaller until it was just a tiny green dot below.

It was most peculiar. He wasn't afraid and he was as comfortable as if he was sitting in an armchair. He looked down and saw the road he lived in. He was so high that the cars and houses looked like toys. Even his house. He wondered if his mother could see him. In fact, she was looking out of the window at that very moment thinking what a strange, big bird there was in the sky. Then she went on with her work.

CHAPTER TWO

Soon Philip coudn't see his town any more and there were fields below. He saw a river sparkling in the sun. The fields became mountains with snow on their tops. He could see the little streams that started in the mountains and joined to become the big river that flowed through the fields. One mountain was so high that Philip's feet touched the shining snow on the top.

And all the time the little round cloud led the way. And the kite followed with its long dragon's tail dancing in the breeze. The mountains went on and on. Philip could feel their icy breath rising up to him. His hands were becoming very cold. For the first time he began to be afraid. Perhaps his hands would slip from the kite and he would fall and fall to the mountains below.

He wished that he was safe at home. Already

he must be more than a hundred miles away from his father and his mother. Where was he going? Would he ever be able to go home again? The more he thought about the danger, the more scared he became and tears began to fill his eyes. He felt one drip on to his foot. And the more he cried, the more his hands and arms grew weaker. Then he realized. He was crying his strength away. He shook his head and the last tears went tumbling through the air. The cold froze them into ice and the sun made rainbows in them as they fell. He smiled at the colours and the strength came back to his arms.

Below him, the mountains grew smaller and there were trees on them instead of snow. Away in the distance, Philip could see a long line of blue. He watched as the kite carried him towards it and he finally saw that it was the sea. There was a small stretch of golden sand and then nothing but water. It was deep blue and crinkled and the sunlight bounced off it with wild flashes of silver and gold.

He looked at the boats that were steaming up and down the coast. The water was very clear and he could see shoals of fish darting past the rocks and through the seaweed. Once, he saw an octopus sitting on the pale sand with its legs rippling from side to side. Philip was so busy watching all the life in the sea that he almost let go of the kite in shock when he felt something land on his shoulder and tap him on the ear. It was a robin.

'Hello,' Philip said.

The robin jumped in surprise at Philip's voice and flew off his shoulder and circled round him singing very excitedly. Philip wondered what a robin was doing here so far out at sea. He was sure that the little bird would not be able to rest on the water like gulls and other sea-birds and he thought that the robin's wings must be very tired. He was right because soon the robin landed nervously on one of his feet. He snuggled himself down on Philip's shoe and held one end of the shoe-lace in his beak so that he wouldn't fall off. He looked up at Philip and it seemed as if he tried to wink one of his bright eyes. Then he tucked his head down under his wing and went to sleep.

'It's as if he knows it's going to be a long journey,' thought Philip.

The kite flew on and on. Now the big red sun was beginning to sink slowly in the West. Philip's father had told him how there is night and day because the earth turns, but as he looked at it now, the sun really seemed to be disappearing into the water. Soon, it was completely gone and in the dark sky Philip could see the stars.

'I wish I could go to sleep like you, robin,' he said out loud.

There was a rustling noise and Philip felt the tail of the kite wrap itself tight round his body and his arms. Now he could go to sleep without falling off. He let go of the wooden cross-piece of the kite. For a moment he was scared that the tail might not hold him but he felt it tighten round him comfortably and he knew that he was safe. He closed his eyes and the gentle swaying of the kite rocked him to sleep.

CHAPTER THREE

When he woke up, the sun was already warming his back. He rubbed his eyes and it took him a moment to understand that he wasn't in his own bed in his own room. It hadn't been a dream – there was the sea below him with the morning light melting the mist that lay above the waves. He felt the kite's tail twitch round him as if it was trying to say something. Perhaps it was tired of holding him. He reached up and held on to the kite. The tail unwrapped itself and fluttered up to its proper position. At once, the kite changed direction.

There was a movement on his shoe and Philip looked down to see the robin waking up. The bird shook his head, flapped his wings and puffed out his lovely red chest. Then he looked at Philip. He still seemed rather scared so Philip gave him an encouraging smile. With a whirr of wings, the robin flew up and perched on Philip's shoulder.

Quietly, so as not to scare him, Philip said, 'Good morning. I hope you slept well.'

The robin gave a little bob and Philip couldn't help laughing because it was just as if the bird had understood what he had said and was giving him an answer. The laugh frightened the robin and he hopped a couple of times until he was further away from Philip's face. He stood on one of the folds of Philip's anorak.

'That looks a very comfy ledge,' Philip whispered.

Again, the robin bobbed as if to say, 'It is.'

Philip managed not to laugh out loud but it was so funny that he had to laugh inside and his shoulders shook so much that the robin bounced up and down. That made Philip laugh even more because the bird had to grip on very tight so that he didn't topple over. The robin's face became very serious and wide-eyed. Finally, Philip couldn't hold it in any longer and he burst out laughing. The robin jumped in the air with fright and started flying round and round.

'I'm sorry, robin. I don't mean to scare you but it's so funny because when I talk you bob up and down as if you understand me.'

The robin had been flying round Philip's head but now his wings stopped. He was furious. He opened his beak as though to say something and then dropped like a stone. He had been so angry that he had forgotten to keep flapping his wings. Philip watched him tumble and roll down through the air. For a moment, he was scared that the robin might go on falling until he hit the sea.

'Flap your wings!' Philip shouted, but even before he had finished saying it, the robin had started flying properly again. Philip watched as the robin climbed up towards him. It was a long, hard struggle and by the time he reached Philip, the little bird was tired. He settled back on the anorak ledge and his tiny red chest heaved up and down.

'I'm sorry,' said Philip gently. 'You can understand what I say, can't you?'

The robin bobbed.

'It's just . . . just . . . I never realized that birds could understand human beings . . .'

The robin bobbed violently and shook his head.

'They can't?' Philip said.

The robin shook his head again.

'Just you?'

The robin's chest swelled out with pride. The red feathers seemed to get redder as if the bird was blushing.

'You're very clever, then,' Philip said. The robin bobbed and put his head shyly under his wing. 'Perhaps you can tell me where we're going.'

The robin turned and pointed with his beak.

Ahead of them, Philip could see two islands. One was very large and was shaped like the letter 'N'. The other one was a small round island – just a circle of bare rock, like an 'O'. The kite dipped its nose and started to cruise down towards the large island. Philip could see a dark green forest and some open fields on one side of the island and some jagged mountains on the other.

So, the robin was right. This was the end of the long journey. But think as he might, Philip just couldn't imagine why he had been carried here so far away from his home. It was magic, all right. But was it good magic, or was it bad magic?

CHAPTER FOUR

Philip came down with a bump. He let go of the kite and it flew just a little way to a narrow gap between two rocks. It settled between the rocks and the long dragon tail curled itself round and round in a neat pile by its side.

The little cloud that had led them safely all through the long journey now sat bouncing on one of the rocks. As it bounced, it changed from black to white and grew thinner and thinner. With a faint sigh, it disappeared, leaving only a damp mark on the rock.

Philip suddenly felt very lonely. The cloud had gone, the kite was very still as if it was deeply asleep, and the robin was nowhere to be seen. He stood up and looked around. He was in a clearing in the forest. Which way should he go? He didn't want to end up lost. There might be wild animals. He had come so far across the sea that he might be in a land where lions or tigers lived. On the other hand, he couldn't just stay here. He made up his mind to be brave and started walking towards the trees.

Just where the path went into the forest, the robin flew down from the top of a bush and landed on Philip's shoulder. The robin's happy song helped to make the forest seem a little less gloomy. Even so, Philip shivered a little. The crooked branches creaked and the shiny, wet roots of the trees reminded him of the octopus he had seen in the sea. The forest echoed with the strange tick-tock music of water drops as they tumbled down from the dark leaves on to the trembling ferns.

The path grew narrower and brambles tried to pull him back. As the forest became darker, the robin stopped singing. He pressed himself against the side of Philip's neck and Philip could feel the little heart beating fast.

They came to a rushing stream with stepping stones across it. Philip had just jumped from the last stone on to the path at the other side when he felt a rumbling in the ground. The robin squeaked and flew into the bushes. The air grew colder and there was the thunder of galloping hooves.

Without knowing why, Philip dived into the ferns and lay hidden under some bushes as the noise grew louder. The ground shook and pounded and big chunks of earth flew through the leaves and branches. He pressed his face to the damp soil and held his breath. The noise stopped. Whoever, or whatever, it was had halted on the path next to where he was hiding. There was absolute silence for a moment, then a growling sound.

Philip twisted his head and looked up through the ferns. Two huge black horses towered above him. The riders were dressed in red robes. They had their backs to him but he knew from the horrible noises they made that they were not men. They were sniffing the air like dogs and then growling to each other. They turned and Philip saw green eyes, black hairy faces, wolf-like snouts and pointed yellow teeth. They sniffed and started to look down towards him as if they had caught his scent.

He heard a flutter of wings and he saw a blur of red fly past him towards the riders. It was the robin. The bird darted and dived just out of reach of the snapping jaws, then landed on the head of one of the horses. Philip's chest grew tight as the rider raised a hairy claw and brought it crashing down towards the robin. At the last second, the little bird flew off and the claw hit the horse's neck. The poor beast snorted and reared into the horse in front. The two riders tumbled backwards but managed to hang onto their horses as they charged towards the stream. The horses leaped the water and Philip stood up to watch as they thundered away down the path with their riders' red robes flying in the wind.

As soon as they were out of sight, Philip ran in the opposite direction. He tripped and stumbled over broken branches on the path and his feet sometimes slid into the huge hoof-prints that the horses had left. He kept running until he could run no further. He sat down on some moss at the side of the path and listened. There was no thunder of hooves, only the drip-dropping of the water from the trees.

The robin flew down and landed on Philip's knee. He let Philip reach out and stroke the feathers on the top of his head.

'Thank you for saving me. You were very brave,' Philip said.

The robin whistled and sang and bobbed so hard that Philip had to smile even though he was still out of breath and rather scared.

'We'd better not stay here, robin. Those horrible things on horses might be back looking for us. Is it far to the end of the forest?'

The robin bobbed and shook his head. He jumped onto Philip's shoulder as he got up and started along the path. The trees were becoming less dense and the light was less gloomy. Streaks of sunlight were shining down through the leaves. Philip was just beginning to feel happy that he could see the end of the forest when he heard a strange noise. It was coming from beyond the trees – somewhere out in the sunshine. He moved closer and listened again. Someone with a most extraordinary voice was singing a song.

CHAPTER FIVE

'Swing, swang, swung, swong
Listen to my swinging song.
Swing low, swing high
I'm as biggest as the sky.'

Philip peered from behind a tree and gasped with amazement. The singer was a small beaver who was flying back and forth on a tiny swing that hung from the lowest branch of an apple tree. A little way behind this tree, there was a cosy-looking cottage. The front door was open and a delicious smell of baking bread floated to Philip on the breeze.

The small beaver started his song again and swung up and down so hard that the whole tree rocked. A ripe apple tumbled from the top of the tree, bounced off the lowest branch, and hit the beaver on the shoulder. The shock made him let go of the swing and he toppled backwards off the seat. He managed to catch hold of the rope with his foot but he suddenly found himself swinging upside-down with his nose an inch above the ground.

'Help, help, I'm falling in,' he shouted.

Philip was just about to dash to the rescue when a large badger rushed out of the cottage, almost tripping over her apron. She was carrying some knitting and, in her speed, she had forgotten about the ball of wool which came rolling behind her out of the front door.

'Now don't make a fuss, Baby B. I warned you about swinging too hard,' she said, dropping the knitting and trying to catch hold of the swing.

'Help,' shouted Baby B and grabbed her apron as he swung past.

The sudden jerk pulled the badger off balance and she fell over. Baby B waited until the swing came level with her again then kicked his foot free from the rope. He sailed through the air and crashed on to the poor badger's tummy, knocking all the wind out of her with a tremendous 'OOUUFFF!'

'Thank you, Mrs Badger,' said Baby B, sliding to the ground. 'You stopped me from getting hurted.'

'Oooh,' gasped Mrs Badger as she sat up slowly, trying to get her breath back. 'Really, Baby B, you do get yourself in some pickles.'

'It wasn't a pickle, it was an apple. It bonked me on the shoulder and I let go and then I was falling in.'

'You weren't falling in, Baby B. You might have fallen off and you nearly fell down but there was nothing for you to fall in.'

'I might fall in my head,' said the small beaver.

'On, Baby B, on. You can't fall *in* your head.'

'A flea could.'

'Now that's enough of your nonsense,' Mrs Badger said, as she got to her feet. 'Oh dear me, oh dear me – look at my knitting. All the stitches are off.'

She picked up the needles and started to slide the stitches back on.

'Oh dear me, Mrs Badger, it's all over the garden,' said Baby B. 'I'll help you. I'm good at helping.'

He ran over to the ball of wool and picked it out of a rose bush. He started to roll it up as fast as he could but it got caught round his leg and the more he tried to get himself free, the more he got tangled up. He turned one way, then the other, and then ran round in circles until he began to look more like a ball of wool than a beaver.

'Help, Mrs Badger, it's trying to knit me.'

Mrs Badger groaned, tucked her knitting into her apron pocket, and patiently began to unwind Baby B. She had just got him free and was about to roll the wool into a proper ball when she saw Philip peering from behind the tree. Her eyes grew wide as he walked towards her.

'Are you . . . are you one of the witch's men?' she asked in a scared, gruff voice.

'I don't think so,' said Philip, 'but I did come here by magic. On a kite, all the way from my home. Under a cloud. And a robin came to meet me and . . .'

'A cloud? A robin?' interrupted the badger. 'You mean, you're the . . .?'

'The saver?' broke in the little beaver. 'It's the saver! Hooray! Hello, Mr Saver. I can help you. I'm good at helping and I'm not scared . . .'

'Hush now, Baby B,' said the badger.

'Oh, go on, please Mrs Badger, please let me help him. Please,' Baby B begged, tugging at her apron.

'We'll see. Now stop making a fuss. First of all, you'd better take this young gentleman to see Mr Edgar at once. There must be some mistake. Oh dear me. Another mistake and the witch will be here tomorrow and . . . oh, dear me . . . first that silly car and now . . . Bless my soul, though, I'm forgetting my manners. What's your name?'

'Philip.'

'Well, Philip, Baby B will show you the way to the Manor. Mr Edgar will want to see you at once. And . . . oh my, there's the robin.' She pointed to the robin on Philip's shoulder. 'So, it's true. You are meant to be the saver. And, oh dear me . . .'

Poor Mrs Badger was now in such a state of tears and fussing that she pulled out her knitting from her apron pocket and, thinking it was a handkerchief, blew her nose on it.

Baby B's eyes grew very large and he started to giggle, but Mrs Badger clapped her hands and said, 'Now off with you both. And take care in the trees near the Manor.'

Baby B started to run as fast as his little legs could carry him and Philip followed. When they looked back, Mrs Badger was still trying to roll the wool into a ball. She was talking to herself and shaking her head and dabbing her eyes with her apron. Philip was going to say something to Baby B but the little beaver looked up, giggled, and set off across the fields as fast as he could go.

Philip didn't have to walk too quickly in order to keep up because Baby B's legs were very short and he had obviously only just learned how to run. Philip watched him scurrying ahead, almost tripping over himself. Once, he looked back to see if Philip was following and immediately tumbled over. He giggled, got up, brushed the dust off his dungarees and rushed on, his legs pounding away faster than ever.

They crossed fields full of corn and Philip noticed that it was ripe and should have been cut weeks before. Whoever farmed this land wasn't taking proper care of his crops. All the hedges they passed were overgrown and filled with trailing brambles and weeds. Fences and gates were broken and a plough stood old and rusty in the middle of a field. Philip was wondering why everything looked so ramshackle and run-down when he saw that Baby B had stopped near a thin line of trees that ran all the way back to the forest.

When Philip reached him, Baby B looked up and giggled, then took a step forward. He looked nervously up and down the line of trees, then stepped back and put his little paw in Philip's hand.

'I'm not scared,' Baby B said and gripped Philip's hand tighter.

'Aren't you?' asked Philip.

'No, I'm not scared because I'm six.' He looked at Philip and then looked down at the ground and said, 'I will be soon. I'm two and a half now but soon I will be six.'

'I expect so. Though you'll probably have to be three, four and five first,' said Philip gently because he could feel Baby B trembling.

'When I will be six, I won't be afraid of the growlers, will I?'

'No,' said Philip. 'Are you afraid of them now?'

'A bit,' said Baby B, taking a step closer to Philip. 'If they eat me I don't like it.'

'The growlers, Baby B – do they wear red robes and ride big black horses?'

'Yes, and they have ever so bigger teeth. And Mrs Badger says that oh dear me if the witch comes they will be even worserer. But you won't let them, will you?'

'Well . . .' began Philip.

'Because you're the saver, aren't you?' Baby B said quickly and he trembled so much that Philip smiled and nodded.

'I feel much braverer with you. We won't run through the trees, will we? If they come, you can bonk them on the head!'

Philip tried to look as if he could think of nothing better than bonking some growlers on the head but he had to try very hard to stop himself running as they walked through the trees. He looked anxiously from side to side for any glimpse of movement and he almost jumped out of his skin when Baby B suddenly shouted, 'Ha, Ha! Silly old growlers. We don't care because we've got the saver.'

'Ssh,' whispered Philip, 'we want to keep it a secret, don't we?'

'Oh, sorry,' Baby B said in a loud whisper and Philip was very glad when they came out of the trees and into the sunshine.

Baby B tugged Philip's arm and pointed to a large building standing on a low hill.

So, that's the Manor, thought Philip. I certainly

hope Mr Edgar, whoever he is, will be able to solve the mystery. Some mistake has taken place, and if we don't sort it out soon I'm afraid that it might turn out to be a very scaring mistake indeed.

CHAPTER SIX

The Manor was as tumble-down and uncared for as the fields had been. The front door was hanging off its hinges, there was dust on the floor and there were cobwebs hanging from the beams. Baby B led the way along a corridor and down some twisting stone steps, then along an even darker corridor and down some even twistier steps.

At the bottom of these steps was a small room. The floor was covered with an old carpet that had holes in it and all the furniture in the room was higgledy-piggledy. There was a huge fireplace with a pile of logs burning brightly. In front of the fire, a very large beaver sat in an armchair. He had a piece of paper on his lap and a pencil in his mouth and he was fast asleep.

Baby B ran across to the fire and lay down in front of it. He was so tired after all his running that he immediately curled up and went to sleep. The robin flew off Philip's shoulder and landed on the large beaver's knee. Philip tip-toed over to the armchair. The sleeping beaver had written some very strange letters on the paper – letters that looked like some kind of old magic spell.

Philip shivered and wondered whether he ought to creep out of this house before it was too late. And yet this beaver didn't seem very frightening. In fact he looked very friendly. His fur was all grey and his kind old face was twitching in his sleep.

Philip coughed politely and said, 'Excuse me.'

The old beaver woke up with a start and saw the robin perched on his knee.

'Mmmmmmmmmmmmm, mmmmmmmmmm,' he began, then realised he still had the pencil in his mouth. 'Drat the pencil! Sergeant Robin, you're back, me lad. Well then, was the mission a success? It should've been – I've been sitting here going over the spell time and time again. Come on, lad, don't just stand there bobbing up and down. Did you bring him back?'

The robin bobbed and whistled, then flew on to Philip's shoulder. The beaver turned and peered at Philip.

'What? Oh, there you are. Splendid. Splendid. Didn't see you there. Come round into the light. 'Fraid the old eyes aren't what they used to be. What with that and me shaky old pins,' he said, tapping his legs, 'I can barely walk to the door nowadays. I'm turning into a dreadful old duffer. Edgar's the name, by the way. Now, let's have a look at you. Bit on the small side, aren't you? Young, too. Bless my soul, what kind of uniform is that you're wearing?'

'Excuse me, Sir,' said Philip, 'I think there must be a mistake.'

'Mistake? Fighter pilot chappie – that's what I asked for. Made it clear to the cloud when I cast the spell. Pilot chappie and his kite. That'll be the ticket to save us, I said.'

'Kite?' said Philip.

'That's right – kite. Airplane. Pilot chappie couldn't save us without a plane to fly, could he?'

'Oh dear,' said Philip.

'Don't tell me it went wrong like last time. Asked for a tank, and what did I get? A dratted old banger of a car that doesn't work. Did you see it outside?' Philip shook his head. 'Useless scrap metal. And now, instead of a full grown pilot, I get a useless whipper-snapper of a lad like you.'

Philip was quite angry at being called useless and he couldn't stop himself saying, 'There's no need to be rude. I didn't want to come here. I was snatched away by your cloud.'

'What's that? What's that?' said the old beaver. 'Raised the fire in your belly, have I? Like to see a lad with a bit of spirit. My mistake – good point. Mind you, I would have got the spell right if I'd had me magic books, but they're all up in me library at Beaver Towers. My fault entirely. Anyway, lad, make your report.'

Philip told him everything. From the moment the cloud came and the wind blew him away from the park, right up to his arrival at the Manor. Mr Edgar nodded and tutted and shook his head all the way through the story.

'Well, well,' said Mr Edgar, 'quite an adventure, eh? Brave lad, too, going through all that and still keeping a sensible head on his shoulders. Well done! Can see the confusion about the kite as well. My fault – should've made the spell plainer. Oh well, no use kicking meself now.'

Philip was just going to ask Mr Edgar how he was going to correct the mistake and send him back home, when the old beaver held up his hand.

'Itching to ask questions, eh, lad? Hold your horses. Bad news always slips down better with a cup of steaming tea. Make yourself comfortable and I'll see about some rations.'

Philip sat by the crackling logs and looked at Baby B sleeping peacefully. Mr Edgar busied himself boiling a kettle on the fire and buttering some scones. Philip was hungry and thirsty but he couldn't help wondering about the bad news that Mr Edgar had mentioned.

Things were bad enough as it was – how could they possibly get worse?

CHAPTER SEVEN

'Well, brace yourself, me lad,' said Mr Edgar as they sipped their tea and ate some scones. 'I expect you saw the fields outside – terrible state, eh? The whole island is going to rack and ruin – the fields, the house. Didn't used to be like this, oh no. I used to live in Beaver Towers – beautiful castle in the mountains on the other side of the island.

'You've heard of the eager Beavers and the busy Beavers, of course?'

Philip nodded.

'Well, the two families joined ... oh ... must be five hundred years ago, and built Beaver Towers. You can see our crest above the main entrance – "Always Eager, Always Busy". We were the eagerest, busiest and happiest beavers you could find.

'Then one dark winter's day three years ago we

were betrayed. A weasel who was a guest in the castle crept into the library and stole one of our books of ancient magic. We beavers are good at magic and my family had the best collection of magic books in the world. Anyway, the sly thief went back to his room and started dabbling with some spells. Very tricky thing – magic. If you don't know what you're doing with it things can go terribly wrong.

'Well, the long and the short of it was that the weasel accidentally magicked up a very nasty and evil piece of work. Oyin is what she's called. The cruellest witch in the whole World of Shadows. The weasel was soon taught a dreadful lesson about meddling with magic. As soon as she appeared, Oyin picked him up with her long bony fingers and tossed him on the fire. I heard his dreadful squeals and my blood ran cold. I searched the castle from top to bottom. Of course, by the time I got to the weasel's room, he had been roasted to a pile of ashes and Oyin had flown out of the window into the depths of the forest.

'I saw the book of magic on the floor and one glance at the open page told me what had happened.

'I spent hours in the library looking for a spell that would undo the dreadful evil, but it was too late. Oyin hadn't wasted any time in the forest. She'd cast her spells and had made nearly a hundred growlers. I suddenly heard their horrible howling and growling coming through the forest towards the castle.

'There was nothing for it but to bail out. I called everyone together and we beat a swift retreat. Down we went, through an old secret passageway that leads from the library out of the castle right to the edge of the forest.

'I took a last look at my old home and saw the hideous green eyes of the growlers peering from the windows. And Oyin herself, standing high on the battlements with her black cloak flying in the wind.'

A tear rolled down Mr Edgar's furry cheek and plopped into his cup of tea.

'Still,' he said, sniffing, 'no point in brooding about the battle that's been lost. We were all safely out of the castle and we set up base here at the old Manor. We rallied everyone to our new HQ – badgers, beavers, rabbits, hedgehogs. Everyone.'

'Did the witch and the growlers come and attack?' asked Philip.

'Attack? Oh, bless me, no. Oyin could only stay for one day. Witches can't stand goodness and there was still too much good around for her liking. She scuttled back to her evil world like the slimy rat she is. She left her growlers to do her dirty work.

'The cunning devils would wait until one of

us was alone in the forest or the fields and then pounce. Each time they caught one of us it meant that there was a little less goodness on the island.

'So the second time Oyin came out of the World of Shadows she managed to stay for nearly a week. In that time she made some more dratted growlers. And the more there are, the fiercer they become. Now they've caught nearly everyone. Two months ago they got my son and his wife – they're Baby B's mother and father.'

'So, Baby B is an orphan, then,' said Philip.

'Not quite – they're prisoners in the dungeons of the castle along with all the others. They are locked up there until Oyin's evil is complete and then she'll throw them in . . .' Mr Edgar nodded at the fire and shivered. 'Now there's just me, Baby B, Mrs Badger, the robin and the three Mechanics left. Hardly enough to stop the weakest witch and certainly no match for Oyin. So tomorrow night when she comes back for the third time she will be able to stay for ever. The end of our home. Even if I had all the magic books from my library I wouldn't be able to match her evil.

'And that's where the bad news comes for you, young 'un. My spells just don't seem to work without my books. I get all the words muddled up. I asked for a tank and I got an old banger. Then I asked for a pilot and his plane and I got you. And the fact is, I just can't think of a dratted spell that will get you home.'

Baby B stirred on the rug and Philip thought how his old dog, Megs, always lay like that in front of the fire at home. Wouldn't he ever see Megs again? Would he never go home and be with his family? He blinked back some tears and looked at Mr Edgar.

'Are you sure?' he asked, trying to make his voice as firm and un-trembly as he could.

'Positive, young 'un. I wish I could give more hope to the troops and all that but the hard truth is that you're stuck here with us. No retreat possible and the enemy just waiting to polish us off.'

Mr Edgar patted Philip kindly. The old beaver and the young boy looked at the fire and each thought of his home. In the silence nothing moved except the reflections of the flames dancing in their eyes.

CHAPTER EIGHT

Philip stopped staring at the fire and looked at the painting of a castle that hung over the mantelpiece.

'Is that Beaver Towers, Mr Edgar?'

The old beaver nodded sadly. Philip stared at the picture and he had the oddest feeling that someone was trying to tell him something. What was it? Something that Mr Edgar had said . . .

'Did you say there was a secret passage into the castle?' Philip asked thoughtfully.

'That's correct.' Mr Edgar turned with a puzzled frown. 'Why?'

'Well . . .' began Philip.

'Now, young 'un,' interrupted the old beaver, 'if you're thinking of bursting into the castle and rescuing all the prisoners – just forget it. The place is crawling with Oyin's dratted watch-dogs. It's a brave thought but you wouldn't stand a chance.'

'I know,' said Philip eagerly, 'but you said that the passageway came out in the library. Could I get in there and bring back one of your books of magic? If it was a book of escaping spells you could magic the prisoners out of the castle and then get the cloud to take us all off the island.'

'By Jove!' Mr Edgar shouted and slapped his knee. 'That's right. It might work. Mean leaving our old island to Oyin, of course, but,' he slapped his knee again,

'He who fights and runs away,
Lives to fight another day.'

All this slapping and shouting woke Baby B.

'Hello, Grandpa Edgar,' he said, jumping up on Mr Edgar's lap, 'I bringed the saver, didn't I?'

'You know what, Baby B, I think you did,' said the old beaver, giving his grandson a hug.

'And I wasn't a bit scared of the growlers when we came through the trees,' added Baby B proudly.

'That's a good lad – you're a chip off the old block. Mind you, it's going to have to be bravery all round from now on. There's a special and highly dangerous mission taking place tonight.'

'Tonight?' said Philip. 'So soon?' His heart had just started bumping in a most alarming way.

'Tomorrow'll be too late. Oyin is due for the third time tomorrow night. It's now or never.' He laid a gentle paw on Philip's knee. 'Frightened, young 'un?'

Philip tried to speak but his throat had gone all dry. He just nodded instead.

''Course you are. I would be if I were in your shoes. Do you want to back out?'

Philip looked in Mr Edgar's kindly old eyes and shook his head.

'That's the spirit, young 'un! Knew you had it in you, the minute I clapped eyes on you.'

Baby B bounced up and down on Mr Edgar's lap and squeaked, 'Hooray!' Then he stopped and asked, 'What's he going to do?'

Mr Edgar put his finger to his lips and whispered, 'Shh! Walls have ears, you know. He's going into Beaver Towers to get one of my books of magic.'

'Can I go, too?'

'Not right into the castle, no. That's a one-man mission. Now, don't sulk,' he said, patting his grandson's head, 'you've got your own important job. You must lead him through the forest and show him where the secret tunnel begins. That's a dangerous enough job for a young beaver like you. Remember, it will be night and the forest will be full of growlers.'

'Will I have to come back all by myself?' Baby B said, shivering at the thought.

'Ah! That's where our brave little robin comes in. No, Sergeant Robin, I haven't forgotten you,'

Mr Edgar said to the bird who flew on to the mantelpiece. 'You did very well in the forest when you rescued our young friend from the growlers. Splendid piece of quick-thinking. Have to put you up for promotion. Now, I want you to go with Baby B and do the same thing for him.'

The robin bobbed and flew down on to Baby B's shoulder to show that he knew what he had to do.

'Good,' said Mr Edgar. Then he turned to Philip. 'Yours is the most dangerous job. The book you want is a big purple one and it should be on the shelves next to the secret door.' Mr Edgar stood up stiffly. 'Well, end of briefing. Any questions?'

They all shook their heads.

'In that case . . . Drat me, wish I could go with you but an old duffer like me would be more trouble than he was worth. But I'll get the Mechanics to drive me over to Mrs Badger's in that dratted car first thing in the morning. Until then – take care and . . . Good Luck!'

Mr Edgar saluted smartly and Philip and Baby B stood up and saluted back. The robin flew onto Philip's head and tried to salute, too, but his claw got caught up in his wing and he fell over.

Philip smiled but he was too nervous to laugh. His mind was full of the night, the forest and the growlers.

CHAPTER NINE

'It's the silliest thing I've ever heard,' said Mrs Badger crossly. 'I just don't know what Mr Edgar can be thinking of, sending you all off into the night like this.'

'It's our only chance, Mrs Badger,' said Baby B. 'The dratted witch comes tomor –'

'Baby B,' Mrs Badger gasped, 'where did you learn that word?'

'Grandpa Edgar says it all the time. Drat the dratted witch – he says . . .'

'Well that's no excuse for you to use it. I've never heard such a thing. Now, upstairs and wash at once while I make you something to eat. You, too, Philip.'

'But we'll get millions dirty again in the forest,' said Baby B.

'That's not the point. I'm not having you going off looking like a couple of tramps. No more arguing. At once!'

Philip and Baby B went upstairs to the bathroom. Philip washed his hands and face, then Baby B stood on a chair in front of the basin and splashed and hummed and spilled water everywhere. He got some soap in his nose and he started sneezing so he put his head in the bowl and made some more splashings.

Philip sat quietly on the edge of the bath. He had a funny feeling in his tummy and his heart was pitter-pattering very fast. He wished he could hum as happily as Baby B.

'Mrs Badger wasn't really angry,' said Baby B, shaking his head and sending even more water flying from his fur. 'It was only pretend angry to make you do smelly things like wash or go to bed.'

'Oh, it's not that . . .' Philip started to say but Baby B went rattling on.

'That's why badgers are good at looking after you because they keep badgering you until you do things.' He pulled the plug out but there was hardly any water left in the basin – it was all over the floor. 'Oh drat – look at all the puggles,' he said and jumped from the chair into the largest pool so that water splashed everywhere.

Philip rubbed Baby B's face and hands with a towel and then gave him a piggy-back down the steep stairs to the kitchen.

All through the meal, Baby B tried saying Philip's name but he kept getting it wrong. He tried 'Pili', 'Lippi' and even 'Fileripip' but most often it came out as Flipip. Philip said that Baby B could call him Flipip because it was easiest and anyway it was a good name.

Baby B's chatter took Philip's mind off his worries. Even so, the flutters in his tummy made it hard to eat much – no matter how many times Mrs Badger came to the table and said, 'Now, eat it all up, both of you.'

They helped wash up and Baby B broke a cup while he was showing Philip how good he was at catching. Mrs Badger was still grumbling about the cup when they all sat down in the parlour to wait for the night to come. Soon, though, her grumbling and Baby B's humming stopped. The fire crackled, Mrs Badger's rocking-chair creaked and the clock tick-tocked steadily.

Philip sat in the window-seat watching the trees in the forest grow blacker as the sun set behind them. The sky became a darker and darker shade of blue and finally he could see the twinkling of stars.

He stood up and hoped that nobody would see how his knees shook.

'Time to go, Baby B.'

The little beaver looked up from his colouring book and his eyes grew very wide. When he tried to say something to Mrs Badger, his mouth opened and a funny squeaking noise came out.

'Come on,' said Philip and took his little paw. 'We'll be all right.'

At the front door, Mrs Badger wrapped a scarf round Baby B's neck and then she kissed them both on the top of the head.

'Be careful,' she said and put her apron to her eyes.

The robin flew down from his perch on the hatstand and landed on Baby B's shoulder. The front door closed behind them and they moved off into the dark.

They had only gone about ten paces when they heard the first distant howl from the depths of the forest.

CHAPTER TEN

At first it was so black that Philip couldn't even see where he was going. Baby B was much better at seeing in the dark and he led Philip along the forest path. Soon, Philip's eyes got used to the night and he could make out shapes in the gloom. There was a mist high in the tops of the trees and the moon glowed through it with a silvery light. Every so often, Baby B stopped and sniffed the air.

Philip didn't like it when they stopped because in the silence the forest seemed to close in on them. Nuts and acorns dropped from the trees, making scaring sounds, and the slight movements of his head as he breathed made it look as if everything was moving.

They crossed the stream where Philip had seen the growlers in the morning. He was just thinking how long ago it seemed since he'd landed on the island, when Baby B stopped suddenly. He sniffed and then whispered to Philip, 'Growlers coming. Into the bushes, quick.'

They left the path and pushed their way through the bushes. The rustling of leaves and the crackling of branches made such a very loud noise that Philip was sure the growlers would hear. Baby B sniffed again and said, 'Down!'

They lay on the ground. There was a long wait. Philip's ears strained to hear the growlers but all he heard was the sound of his own heart beating. How did the little beaver know they were coming? Could he smell them so far away? Philip knew that animals had a better sense of smell than humans. He'd often seen Megs following a scent along the ground, but Baby B was very young so perhaps he'd made a mistake. Philip waited and waited and then decided that it must have been a false alarm.

He stood up as quietly as he could and looked over the bush they had been lying behind. There was a branch in the way so he gently pulled it aside. It made only the softest rustle but two dark shapes on the path immediately turned.

Philip's skin went cold and prickly as two pairs of green eyes looked at him. He froze in fear. There was a growling noise and the green eyes grew larger. The growlers were opening them wide in order to see better. They had heard him but they couldn't see him. He must be hidden in the shadows.

He didn't dare breathe. He didn't even dare to blink. The growlers' eyes seemed to grow larger and brighter and greener. Philip felt as if they were making his head spin. They were telling him to move and make a noise. He felt his knees begin to wobble. Another five seconds and he would have to breathe. He would have to.

On the other side of the path, a large nut made a loud rustling sound as it fell through the leaves, then a thud as it hit a branch. The growlers turned quickly to see what it was. Philip took a deep breath and lowered himself gently behind the bush.

He felt Baby B's paw on his back as though the little beaver was trying to stop him getting up again.

Philip's heart knocked against his ribs and he pressed his face into the pine needles. The seconds passed slowly into minutes. He felt so small and helpless. He remembered the tiny mouse that he had found in the garage one day. He had thought it was funny to see the way it trembled and tried to hide behind a tin of paint but he knew he would never find it funny again.

At last Baby B lifted his paw from Philip's back and whispered, 'They've gone.'

They stood up and brushed the leaves and pine needles off their clothes.

'You were very braver,' whispered Baby B. 'I thought you were going to bonk them on the head.'

Philip shook his head. 'I was very silly, Baby B. I didn't know they were there.'

'Didn't you hearing them?'

'I didn't hear them come and I didn't hear them go.'

'Gosh, you've got funny ears.'

'Boys' ears aren't as good as beavers' ears, Baby B. And I can't smell things a long way off like you, either. Where are they now?'

'Oh, they're millions away. Come on.'

Branches kept poking Philip and brambles pulled at his legs. Wet cobwebs wrapped themselves round his face and he made awful scrunching sounds with every step. Baby B, who was moving almost without making a sound, kept turning round and going 'Sshh!'

Philip tried even harder to be quiet but at once he trod on a twig that broke with a loud snap. The robin started twittering softly.

'Flipip, robin wants to know why you're pretending to be a elephant,' said Baby B.

'I'm not. But my feet seem to like treading on the noisiest things they can find.'

'Take your shoes off,' Baby B suggested.

'I'll get splinters and thorns in my feet.'

'I don't get slinsters and forns in mine. Look.' Baby B held up his foot to show Philip.

'Well, human beings are different from beavers,' Philip said, wishing he could be more like a beaver.

Baby B nodded and looked at Philip. 'Human beaks are a bit funny.'

'Yes,' said Philip, 'I suppose they are.'

Baby B started to walk away and then came back a little shyly. 'Flipip,' he said, 'you're the bestest human beak I've ever met.'

'How many have you met?'

'Only you. But even if I met lots, you'd still be the bestest.'

They decided to go on the path because there would be less noisy things for Philip's feet to tread on. Baby B sniffed and listened hard, then said that there weren't any growlers around. They moved quickly along the twisty path and soon they saw the mountains.

'We see the castle in a minute,' Baby B whispered.

They ran along the edge of the forest, keeping in the shadow. They stopped behind a low pile of rocks and Baby B pointed. In the glow of the misty moon, Beaver Towers looked cold and unfriendly. There were a few lights in some of the windows and Philip could see the shadows of some growlers in the rooms but most of the castle was in darkness. An owl hooted and flew across the moon.

They crossed a small glade to a wall of rock. Baby B pulled some ferns aside and pointed to the stairs going down into the darkness. A strange damp smell drifted up from the hole.

Philip wished he didn't have to go down there.

'There's sixteen steps, Flipip.'

'Thank you Baby B. Will you be all right, going back by yourself?'

'I've got robin.'

'Of course, you have. Well . . . good luck. I'd better get going.'

Philip went down the steps until his head was level with the ground. He looked at Baby B and the robin. How he wished he could go back with them to Mrs Badger's safe, warm parlour.

''Bye Baby B. 'Bye robin,' he said and then, plucking up his courage, he started down the steps.

Fourteen. Fifteen. Sixteen. He was at the bottom.

He looked up and saw Baby B's face peering through the ferns at the top of the steps.

'Good luck,' whispered Baby B.

'Thank you.'

Philip shivered as he heard his whisper slither away into the echoey darkness ahead.

CHAPTER ELEVEN

Philip had never been in such darkness in his whole life. It was like being blindfolded. He could only move by feeling his way along the slimy rock of the walls.

Water dripped from the ceiling and when a drop fell on to his shoulder it was like a finger tapping him. Mr Edgar had said that Oyin had long bony fingers. Perhaps she had come back a day early. Perhaps she was up there in the darkness just waiting to grab him.

He stumbled over loose rocks on the floor and grazed his knee. When he stood up, he wasn't even sure that he was going in the right direction. He half hoped that he would find himself back at the steps and that he would be able to go up through the ferns into the silver moonlight. But he walked on and on and on and he realized that he must still be going towards the castle.

Supposing the growlers had found this secret tunnel? They might have left traps to stop people getting in. They might have dug a huge hole in the ground. At any minute he might fall into it. Perhaps they had put spikes at the bottom of the hole. They might have left a wild animal in the tunnel. Perhaps there was a snake lying in wait on a ledge only a few inches away from where his hand was.

Philip took his hand away from the wall and stood still. If he kept thinking silly things like that, he would scare himself so much that he wouldn't be able to move. He must go on. He must think of other things. He started walking and tried saying the alphabet backwards. Z, Y, X, W.

Something made a flapping noise. Then there was another flap near him. And another. Then there was a loud boom as thousands of wings started flapping. Things were flying past him.

Bats.

He could feel the air moving all round him. He fell to the ground and started crawling. The noise of flapping and squeaking grew less and less as the bats flew away down the tunnel.

He found he could move much faster on his hands and knees. The floor began to slope upwards. He must be getting near the castle now. Then he came to the steps. He stood up and started to climb.

Up, and up, and round and round he went. He was getting puffed so he sat down for a rest. Somewhere below him he heard a footstep on the stairs. He listened hard. Nothing. He got to his feet, went up two steps and stopped. He heard the footsteps climb two stairs and stop. Someone was following him up the stairs.

Philip stood where he was and stamped his feet as if he was going upstairs. When he stopped, he heard some footsteps just round the corner. There was a flutter of wings. The bats? Then something landed on his shoulder and gave him a friendly peck on the ear. It was the robin. Philip felt warm feathers against his neck.

'Is that you Baby B?' he called down the stairs.

'No,' said Baby B's voice.

'Who is it then?'

'No one. It's not me, Flipip. Only it will be me if you aren't angry.

It was so good to hear a friendly voice in the dark that Philip couldn't be angry even though Baby B shouldn't have come.

'I'm not angry,' he said and sat down on the stairs.

He heard Baby B climb the steps up to him and then felt the little beaver jump on to his lap and give him a hug round the neck. Philip hugged him back.

'I expect I was a bit scared in the dark,' whispered Baby B in Philip's ear.

'I expect I was, too,' said Philip.

'Can I come with you into the castle, Flipip?'

'Well, since you're here already . . .'

'It's bestest when there's three of us, isn't it? Me and robin and you?'

'Yes,' said Philip, 'it is.'

They climbed the rest of the stairs together and, in the darkness, they bumped into the wall at the top. Philip knew this must be the secret door into the library. He took a deep breath and pushed.

Slowly, the wall creaked and began to swing open.

CHAPTER TWELVE

Philip peeped through the gap. There was a flickering light from the flaming torch on the wall. He listened. Not a sound. He pushed some more and the gap grew bigger. They were in luck. The room was empty.

Philip tip-toed into the library and Baby B followed. The wall they had pushed open looked like all the others – full of books. Philip took the torch and held it up to the books in order to see better.

'I think this is right, Baby B. Mr Edgar said it was on the shelves next to the secret passageway. Now let's see. A purple book. Green books, blue books, red books, black books but no purple ones. Ah, yes – here. Oh dear. There are two. Mr Edgar only mentioned one. Which one do you think it could be, Baby B? Baby B?'

Philip looked down. Baby B wasn't there. He

turned round and saw to his horror that the little beaver was standing in the open doorway. 'Baby B, what are you doing? Close the door – the growlers might see you.'

'I'm going to find my mummy and daddy,' said Baby B and he ran out into the corridor with the robin flying after him.

'No, Baby B. Come back.' But it was too late.

Baby B was already scampering away. Philip dashed to the door. The little beaver was out of sight. Philip ran along the corridor and saw some stairs leading downwards. He could hear Baby B's footsteps and he called as loudly as he dared. But the footsteps didn't stop.

Philip tore down the stairs two at a time. At the bottom, there was another corridor. It was empty. Philip decided to turn left but he had only gone a couple of steps when he heard Baby B's voice coming from the other direction.

'Mummy, where are you?' Baby B was shouting so loud that he would wake up every growler in the castle.

Philip ran in the direction of the noise. He turned a corner into a brightly-lit corridor. There were suits of armour all the way down one wall. At the far end, Baby B was standing, shouting at the top of his lungs.

'Baby B,' Philip called and the little beaver turned to face him. Philip put his finger to his lips and then beckoned. Baby B shook his head and moved away. He stopped with his back to a large door and shook his head again.

'I want my mummy.'

Philip saw the knob turn and the door begin to open behind Baby B. Evil green eyes shone from the doorway.

'Look out!' Philip shouted but a black claw swept down and grabbed the young beaver by the ears. Baby B screamed as the growler swung him up into the air. The robin flew towards the growler and tried to peck it. The growler opened its horrible mouth and howled as the little bird's beak nipped its nose. The savage yellow teeth snapped and caught one of the robin's tail feathers.

The robin flew on to a suit of armour then dived for another attack. This time the growler was ready. It waited until the last minute then raised its arm and swiped the bird with its claw. The robin crashed against the wall and fell to the ground in a shower of feathers.

There was a moment of silence, then Baby B began to cry. Philip raised his torch over his head and charged along the corridor. The growler took one look at the flames of the torch and darted back into the room.

The door banged shut and Philip heard a key rattle in the lock. He tried the door knob but it wouldn't move. He banged the torch on the door and heaved with all his might but the wood was so thick that he knew he would never be able to break it down.

He heard Baby B's voice calling faintly and he put his ear to the door.

'Run, Flipip, run,' the little beaver was shouting. Then there was a scream and a thud and the voice stopped.

Howls echoed round the castle and footsteps were growing louder. Philip saw a group of growlers come running down a staircase on the right. He bent down and picked up the still robin. The bird's feathers were crumpled, one of his wings stuck out and his chest was stained with a deeper red than usual.

The growlers were nearly there but Philip gently put the robin in his pocket. The leading growler raised its claws ready to pounce. Philip ducked and darted back along the corridor. He pulled quickly at each suit of armour as he passed and they all fell with loud clangs behind him. He turned the corner and saw the growlers tripping and falling over each other as they tried to jump the crashing armour.

He ran along the corridor, up the stairs, then along the hall to the library. He slammed the door shut and pushed a chair against it. Then he dashed to the bookshelves and reached for the purple books.

There was a terrible growling and banging on the door. One of the books fell out of his hand.

The chair began to slide forward as the growlers pushed the door. There was no time to pick up the other book so he dived into the secret passageway.

He pushed the wall and it closed.

A second later he heard the chair go flying as the growlers burst through the door into the library. There were astonished grunts and growls as the evil creatures saw the empty room. Then there was the crash of books and furniture as they began to tear the room apart looking for him.

He held the torch up high and dashed down the steps.

He ran and ran. Down the steps and along the endless wet tunnel he went. He barely noticed the bats that flew in terror from the light of his torch. He was not aware of his tired legs. All he could think of was Baby B's scared little voice shouting, 'Run, Flipip, run.'

He felt the fresh air hit him as he burst through the ferns at the end of the tunnel but he didn't stop.

The branches and brambles of the forest tried to slow him down but he smashed at them with his torch and pushed his legs harder and faster.

When he burst into Mrs Badger's parlour, he saw her get up. He saw her begin to open her mouth. But he didn't hear her scream because he felt the room spin and he fell to the floor.

CHAPTER THIRTEEN

When Philip woke up, he was still lying on the
floor but there was a pillow under his head and a
blanket tucked round him. Mrs Badger was sitting
in her rocking-chair. The robin was lying in her
lap and as she stroked his feathers big tears rolled
down her striped face.

'The growlers have got Baby B,' said Philip.

Mrs Badger nodded. 'The robin told me. The
poor thing has broken both his wings. He's asleep
now.'

'Will he be all right?'

'We must wait for Mr Edgar. He's very clever
at things like that. I'll just put him on a bed of
cotton wool in the kitchen – it's nice and warm in
there. Then I'll make some broth for you.'

Philip felt weak. When he tried to get up, his
legs were very wobbly and his whole body ached.
He lay down again and listened to the comforting

banging of pots and pans from the kitchen.

The broth was hot and tasty. Philip got up and sat with Mrs Badger in front of the fire. She sighed and said, 'Bless my soul' and 'Oh dear me' when he told her what had happened in Beaver Towers. She blinked and blew her nose when he came to the part where the growler caught Baby B. At the end of the story she sat silently staring at the fire.

'What about the word?' she asked at last.

'What word?' said Philip.

'While I was putting the bandage on the robin's cuts he kept saying – 'Flipip knows the word. Flying. Flying. Flipip knows the word.' The poor thing was in a lot of pain. It hurt him to speak but he said it over and over.'

'I can't think what he meant,' said Philip, thinking hard.

'Oh well. Folks say funny things when they're in pain.' Mrs Badger got up and looked out of the window. 'It's nearly morning. Mr Edgar should be here soon. Bless me, but I hope he can do something to help us all.'

Philip sat wondering about what the robin had said. What word did he mean? Something to do with flying. Bird? Wing? Kite? Feather?

The sun was just beginning to peer through the dawn mist when Philip heard a noise coming towards the house. It was a clattery, clanking, clinking sort of sound, mixed with some grunts and shouts of 'Heave Ho!'

Philip got up and looked out of the front door and saw a very old, open car bumping slowly across the fields. Mr Edgar was sitting in it and holding the steering wheel but he wasn't really driving it. Philip could just see three pairs of legs pushing very hard from behind.

The car squeaked and rattled up to the house then stopped. Three hedgehogs in oily overalls rushed round from the back and two of them saluted while the third pulled the door handle of the car. The handle came off in his hand and Mr Edgar had to climb over the door to get out.

'Morning, young 'un,' Mr Edgar said, taking off a huge pair of goggles. 'What do you think of me dratted car? Well done, Mechanics,' he said, saluting the three hedgehogs. 'Fall out and take a rest.'

The hedgehogs took out dusters and started polishing the car furiously.

'They love the dratted thing,' Mr Edgar said, taking Philip's arm. 'I can't get them to stop working on it. Polish, polish all day long. It'd be quicker to walk, even for an old duffer like me, but they'd be so upset. Anyway, enough of that. Did you get the book?'

'I don't know whether it's the right one. There were two, you see. But oh, Mr Edgar, something terrible has happened. The growlers have got Baby B and they hurt the robin. And his wings are broken. And Baby B is a prisoner. And Mrs

Badger said that you might be able to help the robin. But he's terribly ill and he thinks I know a word. But I don't know what it is and . . .'

'Hold your horses, lad,' said Mr Edgar looking very anxious. 'Tell me slowly. One thing at a time.'

Philip told him the whole story and Mr Edgar's old face grew more and more worried.

'That foolish little beaver,' he said when Philip had finished. 'Always was headstrong – that's why I told him he couldn't go into the castle. I just hope . . . Oh well, first things first. I'll see what I can do for our injured robin and then have a look at the book. I just hope, for all our sakes, it's the right one.

'You stay out here – you look as if you need some fresh air. Besides, I expect Mrs Badger is in a bit of a state. I'll have a quiet word with her to cheer her up. Must keep her looking on the bright side, eh?'

Mr Edgar stepped inside the house and winked at Philip as he said out loud, 'It's me, Mrs Badger. Now don't you worry – everything will be all right.'

Philip stood and listened to him chatting away to Mrs Badger as though there was nothing to worry about.

If only that was true, thought Philip.

CHAPTER FOURTEEN

Philip looked at the three hedgehogs fussing round the car. They were blowing on the paint and rubbing very hard with their dusters. The car shone and sparkled so much that Philip was surprised to see that the tyres were flat and that one of them even had a bandage wrapped round it.

'Hello,' he said, walking over to the car. 'I'm Philip.'

The three hedgehogs stopped polishing and saluted.

'Mick,' said the big hedgehog.

'Ann,' said the next.

'Nick,' said the smallest. Then he giggled and hid his face behind his duster.

'He's shy,' the other two said and pushed him behind them.

'Mick. Ann. Nick. Oh, that's why you're called the Mechanics. That's very clever. It's a pity you have to have a girl's name, though,' Philip said to the one called Ann.

'What do you mean? I AM a girl! What a cheek! Just because I work on the car. People always think I'm a boy. Girls are just as good at pushing and polishing. Aren't they?' Ann nudged Mick and Nick and they both nodded.

'Oh, I am sorry. It wasn't that I thought you couldn't do those things,' Philip said. 'It's just that ... you see ... I ... I don't know how to tell if hedgehogs are girls or boys.'

Nick giggled then he chuckled and gasped and hopped around on one foot. Then he slapped his knee and pointed at Philip and then at Ann. He bit his duster but the more he tried not to laugh, the more he did. He rolled on the ground holding his tummy and kicking his legs in the air.

Philip decided it would be best to change the subject so he asked Mick and Ann why the car didn't work.

'Of course it works,' said Mick, 'how do you think it got here?'

'I thought you were pushing it.'

'You don't expect it to come here by itself, do you? It would get lost,' said Ann.

'But what about the engine?' asked Philip. 'Have you tried starting it?'

'Engine?' Mick and Ann said together then looked at each other as though they thought that Philip was being silly.

'Yes, cars have engines that make the wheels turn round. That's why they're called motor cars.'

'Ours is not called that,' said Mick. 'Ours is called Doris.'

'Do you know how to tell if *cars* are boys or girls?' Nick asked giggling.

Philip shook his head and Nick started laughing all over again.

'You don't know much about cars, do you?' said Ann.

'Not much,' admitted Philip, 'but I do know that cars have engines. And I also know that tyres should be blown up.'

'That's what Mr Edgar said. But it just made a hole in it when we tried. Look!' said Ann pointing to the tyre with the bandage on it. 'Perhaps we used too much dynamite.'

'That's not quite what I meant,' Philip said. He thought he'd better change the subject again. 'Would you mind if I sat in the car?'

'Not at all,' said Ann. 'But don't touch anything and be careful you don't scratch the paint when you get in. Come on, chaps. Back to work.'

The Mechanics set to with their dusters and Philip climbed over the door into the front seat.

He held the steering wheel and turned it from side to side. It was very different from his father's car. Philip had often been allowed to pretend he was driving when the car was in the garage. His father had even showed him how to start the car by turning a key. He looked down and saw a key.

Should he try?

It was a very old car but perhaps it still worked. He turned the key and a little red light came on just as it did on their car at home. But when he tried to turn it some more, it wouldn't move. Then he saw a button just above the key. Something was written on it but it was very faded.

He bent down and peered at it – there was an 'S' at the beginning, then two letters that he couldn't read, then 'RT'.

'It must be "START",' he said out loud.

'Pardon?' said Ann, peering over the door.

'Oh, nothing,' Philip said, putting his hands on the steering wheel.

Ann bent down and started polishing again. Philip looked at the button. It was very tempting to try. He leaned forward and put his finger on it. Then he closed his eyes and pushed.

There was a whirr and a clatter then a very loud bang. A huge puff of smoke shot out of the back of the car. The Mechanics jumped into the air, dropped their dusters, and bolted away. Philip saw them dive into a ditch just as the car started to rattle and shake.

It was working. It was jolting and coughing and rocking and wiggling but it was working. There were three more loud bangs and three more puffs of smoke then Philip switched it off. The car bounced a couple of times then stopped.

He stood up and cheered. Three very scared and wet hedgehogs slowly appeared from the ditch. He jumped out of the car and ran over to them.

'It works!' he shouted.

'W . . . w . . . w . . . what did you do to Doris?' asked Mick.

'I just started her,' Philip laughed.

'She was shooting at us,' Mick said. 'You must have made her angry.'

'And you set fire to her,' Ann added. 'Look at the smoke.'

'No,' Philip said, 'that's only because she's old and hasn't been going for a long time. Isn't it good, though? She'll go by herself now. What's the matter? Aren't you pleased?'

The Mechanics didn't look at all pleased. They hung their heads and looked very sad.

'Do you mean we won't be able to push Doris any more?' said Nick and there wasn't the slightest giggle in his voice.

'You won't have to because the engine will do the work.' Philip tried to sound cheerful but he could see that they didn't think it was very good news.

'We like pushing her,' Ann sniffed. 'It's our job. It's what we do better than anything. Pushing and polishing. She's our friend.'

The other two hedgehogs nodded sadly. Philip wished he'd never pressed the button.

'Well . . .' he began slowly. 'Perhaps . . .'

The Mechanics looked up hopefully.

'Perhaps,' he went on, 'it's still better to push her. She is rather old.'

'And she did make lots of noise, so perhaps she doesn't like going by herself,' Mick suggested.

'Yes, and there was all that smoke,' said Ann.

'And the bangs might scare everyone,' Nick said from behind Ann.

'Especially Mr Edgar,' added Ann. 'So perhaps it *would* be best if you didn't tell him about it.'

Philip smiled and looked at the Mechanics. Their overalls were soaking wet and their prickles had bits of weed sticking to them.

'You're quite right,' he said, 'Doris is much nicer when she doesn't make all that noise and all that smelly smoke. I'm sure that Mr Edgar prefers her to be pushed. It's best not to say anything.'

The three hedgehogs jumped up and down and cheered and patted Philip's back.

'That's enough,' Ann ordered after a while. 'Back to work, chaps.'

They rushed off, picked up their dusters and walked towards the car. They touched it gently and then stepped back as if they were a bit scared it might start shaking and banging again. When it didn't, they laughed and set to work polishing more madly than ever.

Philip sat on the grass near them. The Mechanics were so happy that when Nick started to giggle, the other two joined in. The sunlight bounced off the shining car and slid along the threads of a spider's web in the grass.

A fat bee wobbled off the edge of a flower and started buzzing towards the car.

'Go away, please Mr Bee,' Mick said kindly, 'we don't want your dusty feet walking all over our Doris.'

The bee turned round and landed on a pink flower. The flower bent sideways under the bee's weight. A striped caterpillar, that had been climbing the stem, decided that it didn't want to meet the bee. It arched its body and started the long journey back to the ground.

The Mechanics were still polishing half an hour later when Mrs Badger's front door opened. Philip only had to take one look at Mr Edgar's face to know that the news was bad.

He got up and walked towards the house and saw that huge black clouds were rolling towards the sun.

CHAPTER FIFTEEN

'Mrs Badger has just gone out to pick some herbs,' said Mr Edgar as they sat down in the parlour. 'We'll mix them up and give them to the robin. He's very poorly, I'm afraid, and those wings of his are going to take a long time to mend. The herbs will do him good.'

'Did you ask him about what he told Mrs Badger? "Flipip knows the word" – that's what he said.'

Mr Edgar shook his head, 'No. He's much too ill to talk.'

'Perhaps he'll be able to tell me in a couple of days,' Philip said.

'I'm afraid that will be too late. You did what you could, young 'un – but I'm sorry to say that it was the wrong book. Drat it! Never knew there were two purple books. This one's very queer indeed. All the pages are blank. Not a word in it.

Can't think what it can be. Have a look.'

Mr Edgar got up and looked round the room.

'Are me old eyes getting worse or has it got dark all of a sudden? Can't see the dratted book. Can't even see the dratted table.'

It had got darker. Five minutes ago it had been sunny but now it looked almost like night outside. Philip rushed to the window and saw a flash of lightning jump from the black clouds and strike a tree at the edge of the forest. The tree split and fell to the ground just as the thunder roared and shook the house.

The front door burst open and the Mechanics tumbled in. There was another crash of thunder and they screamed and rolled up into three prickly balls.

'Close the door!' shouted Mr Edgar.

The wind was blowing wildly. Huge drops of rain blew into Philip's face. He pushed the door hard and forced it shut.

'Give me a hand to pop the Mechanics under here. They get very scared when there's a storm,' Mr Edgar said, rolling Ann across the floor and pushing her under the sofa. Philip rolled Mick and Nick across the carpet and tucked them in alongside Ann.

Lightning flashed and they heard another tree creak and smash to the ground. Pots and pans rattled in the kitchen and one of Mrs Badger's paintings fell off the wall. The wind whistled down the chimney and tried to blow out the fire. Ash and smoke flew round the room but the flames still burned on the logs and made darting shadows on the walls.

'I don't like the look of this at all,' whispered Mr Edgar. 'This is no ordinary storm. Oyin is behind it, I'm sure. It's a magic storm that she has sent from the World of Shadows. She means to catch us before she comes back to the island tonight. Watch through the window for Mrs Badger. I'll go and fetch the robin in here.'

Philip peered through the window. The rain on the glass made it hard to see. Lightning flashed across the sky and Philip gasped as he saw it light up hundreds of green eyes at the edge of the forest.

'Growlers!' he shouted. 'Quick, Mr Edgar. Growlers in the forest. I saw their eyes.'

'Just as I thought,' Mr Edgar said, laying the robin's bed down by the fire. He hurried over to the window. 'They've come to get us. Quick, lad, lock the doors.'

Philip dashed to the front door and turned the key. He ran into the kitchen and went towards the back door. He was just reaching out for the key when the handle turned and the door began to open.

He stepped back and grabbed a heavy saucepan. A black snout appeared round the door. He raised the pan and was just about to throw it when he saw that the snout belonged to a very wet Mrs Badger.

She banged the door and locked it. Water dripped off her on to the floor and she was panting too hard to speak. Philip took her arm and led her into the parlour.

'Mrs Badger, thank goodness!' cried Mr Edgar. 'Sit down and catch your breath.'

Mrs Badger sat down on the sofa and then jumped up again when three hedgehogs shouted, 'Ouch!'

'Oh dear, the Mechanics are under there,' said Mr Edgar. 'Come and sit by the fire. You're soaked through.'

Mrs Badger sat on a small stool and her fur began to steam as the fire warmed her up.

'Growlers, Mr Edgar,' she panted. 'Everywhere. All round us. I saw them coming and I ran and ran. They must all be out there. I've never seen so many.

'Aye, ma'am, I know. It's all Oyin's wicked work. She sent this storm so that the growlers could have some darkness to hide in.

'Still, it takes a lot of strength to make a magic storm. Even she won't be able to keep it going for very long. If we can hold them off for half an hour, the storm will die out. As soon as the light comes back the growlers will slink away to the castle again. Cowards!' he shouted, shaking his fist at the window.

'What can we do?' wailed Mrs Badger.

'Keep busy. You, ma'am, put all the herbs together in a bowl, chop them up and try to drop a little of the mixture into the robin's beak. The lad and I will keep guard at the window.'

Outside, dim shapes darted through the darkness. From time to time, howls and growls could be heard above the wind and the rain. Green eyes glowed in the gloom and were gone. Long minutes ticked by.

'What do you think they will do?' whispered Philip.

'Attack, of course,' said Mr Edgar, lowering his voice so that Mrs Badger would not hear. 'And soon, too. The thunder and lightning has stopped already. The storm can't last much longer. If only we could think of some way to frighten them.'

There was a loud rattle of tiles from above. Some soot fell down the chimney.

'They're on the roof,' Mrs Badger said and quietly went on trying to coax the robin's beak open.

'That won't do them any good,' Mr Edgar said. 'I built that roof myself. It'll take more than a few growlers to pull it down. And,' he shouted up the chimney, 'you won't dare come down here on to the fire.'

There was a growl and more soot fell on the fire.

Suddenly there was the crash of broken glass

from the kitchen. Philip ran to look. A growler had broken the window and was trying to crawl in. Philip grabbed the frying pan and threw it. The growler yelped and ducked back into the darkness.

There was another crash and the parlour window broke as a stone came flying through it. Mrs Badger screamed and hugged the robin tight. The sofa began to move as the Mechanics shook and shivered underneath it. Mr Edgar took a big poker from the fireplace and rushed across to the window.

'The first one through here will get a sore head,' he shouted. 'Oh, if only I had a tank instead of that dratted car, I'd show you bullies what's what.'

'The car, of course.' Philip ran to the front door and started to unlock it.

'Where are you going? Come back!' called Mr Edgar.

But Philip pulled the door open and ran out into the darkness.

CHAPTER SIXTEEN

A thick mist was swirling round the house. It had nearly stopped raining. If only he could frighten the growlers for a few minutes, the storm would be over. Philip ducked down behind a bush and listened.

There was the padding of paws. Six growlers loomed out of the mist and ran by him towards the house. There were growlings and howlings and snufflings and the sound of breaking glass. Philip dashed to the car, climbed over the door and crouched down.

The rain had left big puddles on the floor but Philip didn't want to move. He was afraid. The minute he sat up a growler might see him.

He peeped over the top of the door. There were terrible noises coming from Mrs Badger's house but he couldn't see any growlers in the mist. He sat on the seat and turned the key. The red light came on. Now to start it – the bangs and smoke would be sure to scare the growlers.

He pressed the button. There was a whirr and a clatter like before but nothing else. The engine hadn't started. He tried again. The engine whirred and clattered and stopped.

As he reached for the button again, he heard the silence. There were no noises coming from the house. No growlings, no tinkling of glass. Just a very scaring silence.

He peered through the mist. Dark shapes were moving slowly towards the car. The growlers had heard the noise. Their green eyes were searching for him in the mist. He pressed the button and the engine whirred and stopped. It must have got wet during the storm. It wasn't going to start.

He looked up. The growlers were in a circle all round him. Their eyes grew larger as they saw him. They bared their yellow teeth and raised their claws. The circle closed in. He could hear low growls rattling in their throats. He felt the car move as one of them jumped on to the back. He pressed the button.

Whirr. Clatter. Bang! The engine burst into life. Bang! Bang! Bang!

The growlers jumped back in shock. There were so many of them that they bumped into each other and fell over. They scrambled to their feet, then tripped and fell again in a howling, whining tumble of bodies.

Philip pushed the gear stick hard and the car started to move forward. It rattled and banged even more now that it was moving. The growlers ran as if they were being chased by a dragon.

Round and round they went in the mist like scared rabbits. Philip turned the wheel and the car chased them. They howled and pushed and bit each other in their hurry to get away.

Philip saw the mist getting thinner. The magic storm was over. He hooted the car's horn and the growlers ran even faster.

All at once the mist lifted and the sun beamed down. The growlers howled, covered their eyes and ran off towards the darkness of the forest. Philip drove after them cheering and laughing. They sped into the trees yelping and yapping. When the last one had gone, Philip turned the car round and drove it back to Mrs Badger's house.

'Well done, young 'un!' shouted Mr Edgar. 'Drat me, that was the funniest thing I've ever seen. Yelping like dratted puppies, they were. First rate idea of yours, that car. Never knew it worked.'

'Thank you,' Mrs Badger said and gave Philip a loving squeeze.

They went inside and Mr Edgar and Philip swept the glass and soot from the floor while Mrs Badger made some tea. The Mechanics rolled out from under the sofa and rushed out to see the car. Soon, their dusters were busy and they were patting the car and saying, 'Well done, Doris. What a brave car you are. You saved us from the growlers.'

Mr Edgar and Mrs Badger sat in their chairs near the fire and sipped their tea. Then they settled down for a nap. Mrs Badger still rocked gently in her chair and Mr Edgar snored and twitched his whiskers.

Philip looked round for the purple book. What bad luck that he had brought the wrong one. Now what were they going to do?

There it was, under a chair. He picked it up and opened it. Mr Edgar had said that the pages were empty, yet the first page had the letter 'P' on it. He turned the first six pages. There was a letter on each page and Philip felt a shiver run down his back.

The six letters were: P-H-I-L-I-P.

CHAPTER SEVENTEEN

'Mr Edgar. Mr Edgar. Wake up!'

'Um? What? Growlers? Drat me, must've dozed off,' he mumbled as he opened his eyes.

'Look – the book. You said it didn't have any writing in it, but it's got my name.'

Mr Edgar rubbed his eyes. 'This is very odd. These letters weren't here when I looked before. They've grown here all by themselves. And look – there are some more letters on the pages at the back of the book: P-I-L-I-H-P. Most peculiar.'

Mr Edgar scratched his head and looked carefully at the letters.

'There's some special sort of magic in this book. Now let me think.'

He looked at the front of the book and then at the back. He got up and walked over to the window and stared out of it.

'By Jove!' he said suddenly and looked at the book again. 'Yes, it does. Well, drat me. The letters at the back are your name backwards.'

Philip looked. Mr Edgar was right.

'But what does it mean?' Philip asked.

'I'm not sure. It's a bit of a puzzle all round. Drat me, what is it? This book is trying to tell us something.'

'Why would it have my name backwards?'

'Well,' said Mr Edgar, 'there's a backwards of everything. Front and back. Up and down. In and out. There's another side of everything. Opposites.'

Mr Edgar paced up and down in front of the fire thinking and muttering. Philip sat quietly by the broken window and looked towards the forest. He tried to think about the letters but he just couldn't stop thinking about Baby B. How was he? Was he scared?

'Well,' Philip said at last, 'I don't know what it means.'

Mr Edgar sighed, 'Nor do I. But I'm sure it's trying to help – trying to give advice or warning.'

'There's only one sure way to find out,' Philip said.

Mr Edgar stopped pacing. 'You mean go back into Beaver Towers?' he said quietly.

Philip nodded.

'You're right, of course,' Mr Edgar said, 'that's why your name is in the magic book. But it's a terrible risk. It's nearly night. Oyin will be back soon.'

'I know. But it *is* the only way, isn't it?'

'Yes, young 'un,' Mr Edgar said, 'I'm afraid it is.'

CHAPTER EIGHTEEN

The sun was sinking behind Beaver Towers when Philip got to the secret tunnel. The forest had been strangely quiet as though all the growlers had gone inside the castle to wait for their evil mistress.

There was smoke rising from the castle and Philip wondered if Oyin was already there. He crossed the glade, pulled aside the ferns and looked down the steps to the tunnel. Half of him wanted to run away but he thought of Baby B. The little beaver was up there in the castle unless the growlers had done something dreadful to him.

Philip didn't know what he could do to help, but at least he could try. He took a deep breath and went down the steps.

He groped his way through the blackness and at last he felt the bottom of the long staircase up to the secret doorway. He started to climb. With every step, it seemed to get colder. His feet grew heavier as if they didn't want to take him upwards. There was evil in the castle.

A voice inside him told him to go back but he forced his feet to climb. At the top, he put his ear to the wall and listened. There was no sound from the library so he pushed gently and the wall swung open.

The room was in a terrible mess. Torn books lay all over the floor. The voice inside spoke to him again stronger than ever. It told him to look for the book and read the escaping spell. Then he could magic himself home, away from the growlers and away from Oyin. He searched on the floor. If only he could find the book, he would be safe.

Far away, he heard Baby B's voice. He couldn't hear the words but the little beaver was shouting. So, he was still alive and he was somewhere here in the castle. Philip got up and walked to the door. The voice inside him told him to keep looking for the book but Baby B's call was stronger even though it was so small and faint.

He opened the library door slowly and looked along the corridor. It was empty. He tip-toed across the corridor, opened a window and looked down.

Far below him was a courtyard. In the middle, a huge fire was burning. Hundreds of growlers were lined up round the walls. In front of the fire stood all the animals that the growlers had taken prisoner. On the other side of the fire was an empty chair raised on some blocks so that it looked like a throne.

Philip knew at once that the chair was meant for Oyin. The growlers were waiting for the witch to come from the World of Shadows and take her seat like an evil queen. Then she would give the word of command and the beavers, badgers, rabbits and hedgehogs would be thrown on the fire.

A small face turned and looked up at the window. It was Baby B.

Before Philip could make a sign to tell him not to say anything, the little beaver's voice was echoing round the courtyard.

'It's Flipip! Flipip has come!'

A growler stepped forward and knocked Baby B to the ground. Two bigger beavers picked him up and tried to hush his sobs and tears. At least, Baby B had found his parents.

All the animals looked up at Philip but the growlers didn't move. They kept their green eyes fixed on the empty throne. It was as if they knew that it was too late for him to do anything.

He suddenly felt very small and afraid. The night had come. The fire was ready. Oyin was already in the castle. He could feel her evil creeping like a mist through the corridors. What could he do? She was so strong and he was so weak. He couldn't save the animals, not even Baby B. All he could do was run away and save himself.

'Philip,' a voice called from behind him.

He turned and came face to face with a boy who looked exactly like him.

CHAPTER NINETEEN

The clothes, the face – everything was the same. It was just like looking at himself in a mirror.

'Who are you?' Philip asked.

The boy smiled with his mouth but his eyes were cold as he said, 'Don't worry. I've come to get you out of this mess. I've found the book. Come and look.'

The boy walked slowly into the library and pointed. The purple book was on the table.

'Let's hurry,' the boy said, 'Oyin will be here soon and it will be too late. We must get home. I'll say the spell. All you have to do is say "yes" to me.'

'But who are you?' Philip asked again.

The boy smiled his icy smile. 'I'm part of you. And if you don't mind my saying so, I'm the sensible part of you. If you'd listened to me on the stairs, we wouldn't be here taking silly risks.

You don't want us to end up on the fire, do you?'

Philip shook his head.

'Well come on, then. Say "yes" and let's go home.'

'But Baby B . . .' Philip began.

'He's just a silly little beaver. He's a prisoner because he was stupid and didn't listen to you. And what's worse, he almost got you caught, too. Don't waste your pity on him.'

The boy was right. All he had to do was say 'yes' and he would be home. And yet . . . something was not quite right.

The boy was looking hard at him and Philip could feel the word 'yes' filling his brain.

'Come on. Come on,' the boy was growing angry. 'Just say the word. You know the word.'

The word! The robin had said that, too. The robin had told Mrs Badger, 'Flipip knows the word'. If only he could think. If only he could get the boy to do something else – just long enough to give him time to think.

'All right,' Philip said, 'I'll say the word. But only if you can write down my name.'

'Why should I do that?' the boy asked angrily.

'So that I'll know you really are part of me. It's a hard name to spell. It took me ages to learn it. If you get it right, I'll believe you.

'You promise you'll say the word,' the boy said, picking up a piece of paper from the floor.

Philip nodded.

'Good. Then we'll leave these wretched islands and go home,' the boy said as he bent over the table and started to write. He held the pencil in his fist and he wrote slowly like a baby. Philip felt himself begin to think clearly again.

He thought of Mr Edgar, Baby B, Mrs Badger. They were his friends. He couldn't just leave them on this island.

The island. That was funny, the boy had said 'islands'.

Philip had forgotten that there were two. There was the big one shaped like an 'N' and there was the little round one by its side. Fancy forgetting the little one. He had seen it from the kite when he had . . . when he had been flying.

'Flipip knows the word. Flying.'

Of course, that was the word that the robin meant. The islands spelt 'No'. And yet the boy who looked like him was trying to make him say 'yes'.

Yes, to what?

'Finished,' the boy said and Philip's thoughts were cut short. The boy looked at him with his cold, staring eyes and Philip's brain was filled with the word 'yes'.

'I've written our name down. Now all you have to do is say the word.'

The word was hurting Philip's head.

'Wait a minute,' he managed to say. 'Show me the name. I want to see if you've got it right.'

The boy passed the piece of paper across and

laughed, 'Of course, I got it right. It's my name, as well as yours.'

Philip bit his tongue to stop the word 'yes' from coming out, then he looked at the paper.

In big straggly letters, the boy had written – P-I-L-I-H-P.

'It's wrong!' Philip shouted. 'It's backwards. You're not me.'

'I am,' said the boy, 'Say it. Say "yes" to me.'

Philip's head was pounding. His lips were beginning to move. The boy was trying to pull the word out of him. He could feel it coming. He closed his eyes and fought. Baby B, Mr Edgar. He loved them. He wouldn't leave them just to save himself. He wouldn't say what the boy wanted.

Philip felt as if he was screaming but the word came out in a whisper, 'No.'

The pain in his head stopped.

The boy stepped back and his face grew so pale that Philip thought that he could see right through the boy's skin to the bones.

'What did you say?' the boy asked and his voice was changing. It was becoming crackly and grating.

Philip filled his lungs and shouted with all his might, 'NO!'

The room shook and a wind began to howl through the door. A blood red light glowed round the boy. Books started to fly through the air.

Philip backed against the wall to stop himself being blown to the ground. He could feel the air burning and freezing. He wanted to close his eyes but he couldn't.

The boy was growing taller and his face was beginning to melt. The skin was becoming older. The eyes were turning yellow. The mouth was filling with broken teeth. Ugly lumps bulged on the skin. It was Oyin.

'Curse you. Curse you!' screamed the witch. She held up her twisted hands and pointed her long bony fingers at Philip.

He pressed himself against the wall as she stepped towards him. Green fire flashed in her slit eyes.

'I'll teach you,' she hissed. Her foul breath oozed round his face. 'I'll teach you to say No to me. You've ruined everything. I could have been queen here, but now . . .'

The library window flew open and Oyin turned and listened. Philip couldn't hear anything but his ears hurt as if a loud voice was booming through the room.

'I'm coming, Master,' Oyin said and began to float towards the window as if she was being pulled by some awful force. 'I'm coming. I'm coming.'

She grabbed hold of one of the bookshelves to stop herself being pulled any further. Her nails dug into the wood.

'I could have been queen!' she screamed. Her

eyes filled with hatred and she threw herself towards Philip. Her sharp fingernails flashed in front of his eyes. Then she was pulled away again. She grabbed the window frame but the force was so strong that the wood split.

Oyin went spinning out into the darkness with a long terrible shriek that echoed through the whole castle.

CHAPTER TWENTY

As Oyin's shriek faded away, Philip heard howlings, yelpings and whining coming from the
courtyard.

He ran from the library and looked out of the
window. Sparks were flying up into the air. Down
below, the growlers were running round madly.
They were jumping into the fire and pulling others
in after them. The flames leaped higher and black
smoke filled the courtyard. In less than a minute,
the last growler had been pulled on to the fire
and the dreadful noise had stopped.

By the time Philip had found his way down all
the stairs to the courtyard, the fire had died and
the smoke had cleared. A group of the animals
grabbed the throne that had been meant for Oyin
and they threw it on the ashes.

'Flipip!' shouted Baby B, jumping up and
putting his arms round Philip's neck.

'Hello, Baby B, are you all right?'

'Yes and the growlers aren't. They all got burneded up like toast. And they were horrible and they put us in the prison. And my mummy and daddy was there. And I got my clothes dirty but it doesn't matter. And I wasn't scared, just a bit. Why did you do that horrible scream, Flipip?'

'That wasn't me, Baby B. That was Oyin. She tried to come here for ever but she couldn't. So she had to go back to the World of Shadows. And when the growlers knew that they got scared and didn't know what to do.'

'Hooray!' Baby B bounced up and down in Philip's arms. 'And if they didn't jump on the fire, you would bonk them on the head. One of the growlers bonked me when I saw you but I didn't cry much, did I?'

'No, I thought you were very brave,' Philip said and gave Baby B a big squeeze.

Suddenly, there came a rattling noise, then some loud bangs and the hooting of a horn. The old car turned the corner and started over the drawbridge towards the courtyard. Mr Edgar was driving. He was wearing his goggles and was bouncing up and down as the car banged and jerked and sent out huge puffs of smoke. The three Mechanics and Mrs Badger were sitting in the back with their paws held over their eyes.

'Out of the way,' shouted Mr Edgar and he honked the horn. 'How do you stop this dratted thing?' he yelled as the car began to clatter and clang round the courtyard.

The animals jumped in the air and ducked into doorways to avoid being run over by the rattling monster.

'Run for your lives,' Mr Edgar gasped as he tried to steer the car away from the walls. 'This thing has gone mad. Help! Hold on to your hats. OOOH!'

The car went round and round in circles, banging and smoking. There was one final bang and the car began to slow down. At last it rolled to a stop and Mr Edgar clambered out.

'Drat me,' Mr Edgar said, wiping his brow, 'the beast went wild. It wouldn't stop, no matter what I said to it. Mind you, it was quite a thrill, eh Mrs Badger?'

Poor Mrs Badger shook her head and even her black stripes seemed rather pale.

'Wonder why it stopped?' Mr Edgar said, tapping the car with his foot.

'Perhaps it ran out of petrol,' Philip said.

'Drat me. That means we won't get it going again. Got no petrol on the island. What a shame. Never mind, it's probably safer when the Mechanics push it.'

The three hedgehogs stopped shaking and took their paws from their eyes.

'You mean we can push Doris like before?' Ann said.

Mr Edgar sighed and nodded.

'Hooray,' shouted the Mechanics and they jumped out of the car and started to polish it at once.

'Well, young 'un,' Mr Edgar said, putting his arm round Philip's shoulder, 'it seems that you were the saver, after all. Dashed fine job. Could smell fried growler all the way here and we saw old Oyin go shooting through the air like a fat rocket. Come on, everyone. Let's go into dear old Beaver Towers and make ourselves at home again. I want to hear how this young lad got rid of Oyin for us.'

CHAPTER TWENTY-ONE

Everyone set about cleaning Beaver Towers. They scrubbed and rubbed and dusted and swept. Of course, the Mechanics were best at this work because they had had lots of practice. They bossed everyone around and each time an animal thought it had finished a job, one of the Mechanics would arrive and say, 'It's not shiny enough. Polish harder.'

Baby B fell into a bucket of soapy water and for an hour he blew bubbles every time he tried to speak.

Soon Beaver Towers was looking spotless. Fires glowed in every fireplace and the kitchen began to smell of good things cooking. Mrs Badger went back to her house and brought the robin in his bed of cotton wool. Philip and Baby B sat and stroked the robin's feathers and after a while he opened his eyes.

'Our little robin is doing very well,' said Mr Edgar as he mixed up some more herbs. Philip and Baby B were left in charge of feeding him. Baby B spilled most of the mixture on his dungarees but the robin ate as much as he could and soon his eyes began to shine again.

They all sat round the long table in the main hall and ate a delicious meal. Then they pulled up their chairs in front of the fire and started to talk. Philip told them what had happened in the library and they listened and shivered as he described what Oyin had looked like.

'By Jove,' Mr Edgar said, 'so the robin was right. You did know the word. I should have guessed, of course. Evil things can't bear to have someone say "no" to them. Quick thinking that, lad. I think we all ought to give our young friend three cheers.'

The three cheers were long and loud and Philip was so pleased and embarrassed that he didn't know where to look. Baby B liked doing the cheers so he started another three and everyone agreed that Philip deserved them.

Then Baby B said it was his turn and he started to make up stories about how he had bonked sixteen growlers on the head and had jumped out of a tower on to Oyin. The other animals smiled and nodded and said 'Well done' and Philip led everybody in three cheers for Baby B.

When they finished cheering, Baby B climbed up on Philip's knee. The little beaver wriggled around to make himself comfortable, put his thumb in his mouth, and fell asleep.

The animals wanted Philip to tell them where he came from. He told them about his school and his friends and about the town. They asked lots of questions about cars and trains, especially the Mechanics who wanted to know who kept them all clean. Then he told them about his home, and about Megs and how he took her for walks and how she liked to sleep in front of the fire. Last of all, he talked about his mother and father, and the more he talked, the more homesick he became.

There was a grey early morning light outside the window when he finished. They all sat quietly looking at the last few flickers of the logs on the fire.

'Mr Edgar,' Philip said softly, 'I want to go home.'

'Of course you do, young 'un,' Mr Edgar said, 'and drat me, you deserve to. I'll just nip upstairs and get my book and we'll send you off straight away.'

While Mr Edgar went to get the purple book, Philip slipped Baby B off his lap on to a chair and said goodbye to everyone. He gave the Mechanics a special pat on their hands, then he hugged Mrs Badger.

'Goodbye Philip,' she whispered, 'and take care.' She dabbed her eyes with her apron.

He gave the robin's feathers a last stroke and the bird managed to open his beak and make a cheerful goodbye chirrup. Then he went over to Baby B who was fast asleep on the chair.

''Bye Baby B,' he said gently and kissed the top of his head. Baby B twitched his nose and turned over in his sleep.

Philip and Mr Edgar walked out of Beaver Towers, across the drawbridge, and down into the forest. They walked slowly because Mr Edgar's legs couldn't carry him very fast but Philip didn't mind. He enjoyed listening as Mr Edgar told him about the happy days he had spent in the castle when he was young.

'And now, thanks to you,' Mr Edgar said, 'I can look forward to a happy old age in me own home. Hmm, just smell the flowers and the leaves. The whole island smells cleaner now those dratted growlers have gone.'

Philip breathed deeply and he knew that he would always miss the island and the friends he had made there.

At last they came to the clearing where Philip had landed. He pulled the dragon kite out of the rocks where he had left it and Mr Edgar opened the book and started saying the spell. The cloud began to form on the top of the rock. It grew stronger and stronger and when it was fully formed it bounced off the rock into the air above Philip's head. The kite's tail twitched.

'Well, young 'un,' Mr Edgar said, taking Philip's hand in his paw, 'I don't know what to say. Drat me, me old eyes are getting worse all the time. Look at them now, filling up with water. Must be the cold air. Anyway, lad, thank you. And safe journey.'

A tiny voice sounded in the distance – 'Flipip!' Baby B came tumbling into the clearing. He picked himself up and ran to Philip. He jumped up and gave Philip a hug and pressed his cold nose against his neck.

'Don't go,' Baby B said.

'I've got to, Baby B,' Philip said, putting him down on the ground.

'That's right,' said Mr Edgar, taking the young beaver's paw and holding it tight. 'Philip must go home. But perhaps he'll come and see us again one day. Eh, Philip?'

Philip nodded but he didn't dare to speak in case the tears started to fall.

'Hold tight,' Mr Edgar said and then he finished saying the spell.

The old beaver closed the book and picked up his grandson in his arms.

The wind began to blow. The cloud began to dance in the air and Philip could feel his feet leave the ground.

'Goodbye,' he called.

Baby B waved a small paw and Mr Edgar blinked his old eyes.

'Goodbye,' they said.

The kite rose in the air and soon the two beavers were just tiny dots below. The sun shone brightly and Philip felt the kite change direction.

He was going home.

Choosing a brilliant book
can be a tricky business...
but not any more

www.puffin.co.uk

The best selection of books at your fingertips

So get clicking!

Searching the site is easy – you'll find
what you're looking for at the click of a mouse,
from great authors to brilliant books and more!

Everyone's got different taste . . .

I like stories that make me laugh

Animal stories are definitely my favourite

I'd say fantasy is the best

I like a bit of romance

It's got to be adventure for me

I really love poetry

I like a good mystery

Whatever you're into, we've got it covered . . .

www.puffin.co.uk

Read more in Puffin

For complete information about books available from Puffin – and Penguin – and how to order them, contact us at the appropriate address below. Please note that for copyright reasons the selection of books varies from country to country.

www.puffin.co.uk

In the United Kingdom: Please write to Dept EP, Penguin Books Ltd, Bath Road, Harmondsworth, West Drayton, Middlesex UB7 ODA

In the United States: Please write to Penguin Putnam Inc., P.O. Box 12289, Dept B, Newark, New Jersey 07101–5289 or call 1–800–788–6262

In Canada: Please write to Penguin Books Canada Ltd, 10 Alcorn Avenue, Suite 300, Toronto, Ontario M4V 3B2

In Australia: Please write to Penguin Books Australia Ltd, P.O. Box 257, Ringwood, Victoria 3134

In New Zealand: Please write to Penguin Books (NZ) Ltd, Private Bag 102902, North Shore Mail Centre, Auckland 10

In India: Please write to Penguin Books India Pvt Ltd, 11 Panscheel Shopping Centre, Panscheel Park, New Delhi 110 017

In the Netherlands: Please write to Penguin Books Netherlands bv, Postbus 3507, NL–1001 AH Amsterdam

In Germany: Please write to Penguin Books Deutschland GmbH, Metzlerstrasse 26, 60594 Frankfurt am Main

In Spain: Please write to Penguin Books S. A., Bravo Murillo 19, 1° B, 28015 Madrid

In Italy: Please write to Penguin Italia s.r.l., Via Felice Casati 20, I–20124 Milano

In France: Please write to Penguin France S. A., 17 rue Lejeune, F–31000 Toulouse

In Japan: Please write to Penguin Books Japan, Ishikiribashi Building, 2–5–4, Suido, Bunkyo-ku, Tokyo 112

In South Africa: Please write to Longman Penguin Southern Africa (Pty) Ltd, Private Bag X08, Bertsham 2013